Much Too Much Birthday

by J. E. Morris

Penguin Workshop
An Imprint of Penguin Random House

For you, on your special day. Happy birthday!-JEM

PENGUIN WORKSHOP
Penguin Young Readers Group
An Imprint of Penguin Random House LLC

Copyright © 2018 by Jennifer Morris. All rights reserved. Published by Penguin Workshop, an imprint of Penguin Random House LLC, 345 Hudson Street, New York, New York 10014. PENGUIN and PENGUIN WORKSHOP are trademarks of Penguin Books Ltd, and the W colophon is a trademark of Penguin Random House LLC. Manufactured in China.

Library of Congress Cataloging-in-Publication Data is available.

ISBN 9781524784461   10 9 8 7 6 5 4 3 2 1

Much Too Much Birthday

by J. E. Morris

Maud was very excited. Today was her birthday, and she had invited all her friends to help her celebrate.

"The guests will be here soon," said Mother. "Come help me decorate the cupcakes."

"There are only twelve," said Maud.

"That's right. One for each of your classmates," replied Mother.

"But what about my friends from dance class?" asked Maud.

"And tae kwon do, and the playground, and pottery class, and Camp Fuzzy Bunny?"

"Oh dear. How many people did you invite?" asked Mother.

"Yes! Isn't it wonderful? Big birthdays are the best birthdays!" said Maud.

"It's going to be crowded," warned Mother.

"Don't worry, you can never have too much birthday!" said Maud.

"Where are you going?" asked Maud.

"To buy more cupcakes," said Mother.

"Don't worry," said Maud. "You can never have too much birthday!"

But when Maud stepped outside, she wasn't so sure.

Oh . . .

PIN THE TAIL ON THE DONKEY

Everywhere Maud went, she was *squeezed* . . .

squashed . . .

This wasn't at all what Maud had expected. Her tummy was queasy, and her head felt all floaty.

Quietly, Maud slipped behind the bushes.

Behind the bushes was a nice quiet place where Maud could be alone.

At least she thought she was alone until she heard a small voice.

"Simon, what are you doing here?" asked Maud.

"Eleanor doesn't like big parties," said Simon. "I'm keeping her company."

Maud kept Eleanor company, too.

"It's cupcake time," said Maud.

"I love cupcakes," said Simon.

"Me too," said Maud.

"But what about Eleanor?"

"Maybe we could all join the party together," said Maud.

The cupcakes were delicious.
Even Eleanor approved.

"Eleanor has had enough," said Simon.
"Okay," said Maud. "I'll see you later."

Maud had an idea.

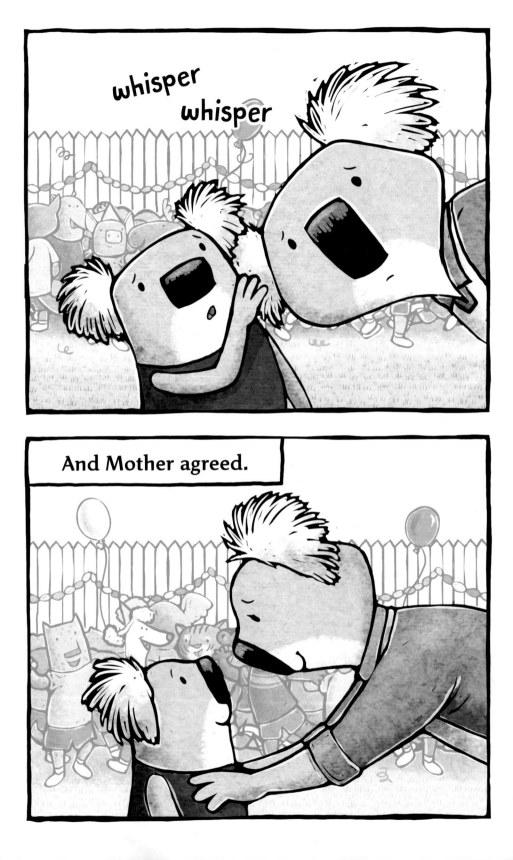

Later that afternoon, after all the other
guests had gone . . .

Maud, Simon, and Eleanor had a
tiny little birthday party.

And it was the best!

Note to Caregivers

Birthday parties are exciting events for children. As parents and caregivers, we want to make our child's special day a happy and memorable one. But some children aren't ready for huge celebrations. Some children, especially the very young and those with sensory sensitivities, can find parties overwhelming. It can be even more daunting when they are expected to be the center of attention.

Know your child and plan accordingly. Some children, like Maud, think they want a huge party but may not understand what that actually entails. Talk with your child before their big day and find a plan that makes everyone happy.

If children do find themselves in an overwhelming social situation, finding a quiet spot to take a break from the commotion can help alleviate their anxiety. Gently encouraging them to participate for small periods of time can help desensitize them to situations they find uncomfortable.